D0119419

97

GW 00584703

A Christmas Child

MELVYN BRAGG

A
CHRISTMAS
CHILD

Illustrated by Brian Campbell

Hodder & Stoughton
LONDON SYDNEY AUCKLAND TORONTO

To Piers Plowright

B367492

British Library Cataloguing in Publication Data

Bragg, Melvyn
  A Christmas child.
  1. Jesus Christ. Nativity
  I. Title   II. Campbell, Brian
  232.9'21

  ISBN 0-340-51039-0

Text copyright © Melvyn Bragg 1976, 1989
Illustrations copyright © Brian Campbell 1989

First published in this edition 1989

All rights reserved. No part of this publication may be
reproduced or transmitted in any form or by any
means, electronically or mechanically, including
photocopying, recording, or any information storage
and retrieval system, without either prior permission
in writing from the publisher or a licence permitting
restricted copying. In the United Kingdom such
licences are issued by the Copyright Licensing Agency,
33–34 Alfred Place, London WC1E 7DP.

Published by Hodder and Stoughton Children's Books,
a division of Hodder and Stoughton Ltd,
Mill Road, Dunton Green, Sevenoaks, Kent TN13 2YA

Photoset by Rowland Phototypesetting Ltd,
Bury St Edmunds, Suffolk

Printed in Great Britain by T.J. Press (Padstow) Ltd,
Padstow, Cornwall

Gwasanaeth Llyfrgell Gwynedd

B 28-11-89

Gwynedd Library Service

Chapter I

T HE SNOW STOPPED IN CHRISTMAS WEEK—BUT ENOUGH HAD already fallen to hold. Everyone wanted it to hold over the festival. It felt lucky. It felt, all were agreed, like a Christmas from long ago.

Few noticed the young couple who came in from the country on the early afternoon bus on Christmas Eve. They were very ordinary. She would have a child very soon, but a large black coat helped disguise that. He had a desperately eager look, swinging the two cheap brown suitcases, one in each hand, so easily that they seemed empty; and indeed there was little enough in them. The driver pointed out the bus-station and they went there to deposit the cases in the Left Luggage.

"She was in a trance, poor little mite," George Robinson, Bus-Station Manager, said later. "You could tell she didn't want to be where she was. And you could tell what sort of material *he* was made out of! Poor little lass, she couldn't have been more than sixteen or seventeen. He didn't seem to want to own her. And such a nice bit of a lass. He couldn't make up his mind how long to leave his cases, so I was forced to charge him for an all-day ticket that could have been a waste of 20p. But she said nothing. Lovely features."

When they came out of the left-luggage office, Joe saw the cafe, the Spotted Cow.

"We always used to go in there," he said, "a big gang of us. Saturday afternoon after the pubs closed, for egg and chips." He glanced at his wife and she closed her eyes against the stricken look on his face. "We could go in if you like for a cup of tea, coffee, cold meat, a sandwich, they've got it all in there."

She nodded and he walked ahead of her across the street

which was a dark gash between the white banks of snow on the edges of the pavement. Timidly, she followed, some paces behind, looking fearfully to left and right for the traffic, a country girl.

"I remember your face," said Mr Ismay, the owner of the Spotted Cow, as Joe stood before him, daring to be identified, "but your name just slips my mind. Two coffees?"

"And all the trimmings," said Joe, lighting a cigarette, blushing a little as Mary came up quietly behind him. "I used to get in here Saturday afternoons."

"It *is* busy then," Mr Ismay agreed. "Toast, is it? And jam or marmalade?"

"You've extended it on a bit," said Joe, nodding wistfully at the new long room. It felt unfamiliar and less cosy.

"That was some time ago. Is the young lady with you?"

"The wife."

Mr Ismay smiled as he handed over the coffees and toast and watched them closely as they carried the awkward cups and plates to a corner table near the juke box.

"She had that look about her that they all have when they know it's about due," he said later. "When I was in farm-work it was the same with beasts. You could always tell when they were going to drop the calf or the lamb, you know. There would be that quietness about them." He thought about the farm more and more as he grew older and sometimes dreamed of returning to it.

It was rarely that Mary had been in a cafe for an inessential cup of coffee and she relished it. Her family was poor and so big that soon after her birth she had been shunted off to a great-aunt and largely brought up by her in the remote hill village to which Joe had come a year ago, driven to farm work by the closing up of the building trade.

She was sixteen, shy, somehow lost in that tiny village, only now beginning to look attractive. Joe had noticed her and talked to her and they had begun to go together. She looked at him now, hesitantly, over the rim of the thick white cup: if only she could calm him down—but what could she say?

"It *can't* be mine," she heard his frightened denial again and again, day and night. "We didn't—we didn't *do* anything."

"There was nobody else," Mary replied—and he knew that was true, but "We can't have made—you know." His innocence was accompanied by an ignorance which always believed the worst happened. Besides he had wanted her and she him: in his unsullied heart this was somehow proof enough. The child was in her and it would be born. That was the fact and he was ashamed.

He could go back to his own part of the county, that was his first thought—to the west coast where the coal mines, now closed down, went out under the sea. But that would be failure. He had disliked the grim town where his parents got drunk and quarrelled in the streets and his brothers gathered on corners to pick out victims for the night's torment and fighting: he did not want to go back. He was out of place there. They laughed at his simplicity, his "daftness". Besides, he loved Mary.

Now, near her time, when panic had set in, he had insisted that she follow him from the village down to this market town in which he had found independence and friendliness for a few months. They all said he was mad to leave the village and take her away from her home in that condition —and he suffered under their accusations.

But there was nothing for it. There was a compulsion— he could not explain it, in some way to stand and be counted. He had to go: and she followed without reproach. Why was he so restless and unhappy now? He could not understand it. Sometimes he thought that he might hate his wife and hate this strange child which was due so soon: and the idea of hating Mary drove him to a wilder misery of self-disgust. He could not cope with that idea. Because he loved her, surely.

Children had put a carol on the juke box and its comforting, sad, long-known verses had taken both of them to a reckoning of the past, for they had first met the previous Christmas at the village dance. When the record came to an end, Joe jumped up—so abruptly that the coffee slopped over the cup and even over the saucer. He looked around to make sure no one had seen and gave a nervous grin of relief when Mary took out her white handkerchief to mop the table.

"I'll see what they've got," he said and went across to the gaudy music-machine. Three for 50p. He studied the lists carefully. This was his chance to say something to her. The song would be his interpreter. Finally, he made his choice.

"The first one's for you," he muttered awkwardly. "Another coffee?"

"No, thank you."

"I think I will." He nodded, acknowledging the aptness of the music, and moved away from her as the song began. She bit her lips not to cry. They had been dancing together and he had asked her to go to the pictures on Boxing Day. This was the song from the film. She hummed it inside her

head as she often did. The words said what she had felt for him then and since.

"Real slate," he pointed to the walls. "Real Cumberland slate that, Mr Ismay was just telling me. Cost a bomb." He lit another cigarette and slung himself onto the chair beside his coffee. "This is the place to be on Christmas Eve. The shops, pubs, a dance—all that."

"We have to find somewhere to stay."

"I'll fix it. Mrs Fell will have me back like a shot. She said I was her best lodger. Any time, she said. You'll like her" —his private and inexplicable uneasiness was goading him once again—"better than that old auntie of yours anyway."

"She was kind to me."

"She treated you like a servant."

"I didn't mind."

"Well, *I* did. My wife's nobody's servant." He leaned over and patted her hand with a borrowed gesture. He had seen a detective do that, weekly, on television. She wanted to lean out and take him in her arms and comfort him: but it was not a thing she would do, nor would it be welcomed; and the bulk of the unborn child was between them. Her arms felt stumpy and weak, beside the solid centre of her body.

"Tell me you love me," she wanted to say, but dared not.

"Why am I so miserable?" he wanted to ask her and did not.

Silently they sipped the milky coffee to the sound of their old tune. "Thank you," she said.

He smiled. "I thought you might remember," he said. "Cheer up." He raised the cup to her.

They finished the coffee and both felt it was time to go, afraid to seem spongers.

"I'll tell you what—you look round the shops, I'll go down and see Mrs Fell and I'll meet you back here at half past five. You can tell it's half past, the hooter goes at the factory."

"I'd rather come with you."

"Look round the shops. Enjoy yourself. Besides, it'd be better if I went on my own."

"Why?"

"Because I know her, you see. She knows me." He looked very decisive. Mary did not persist.

"Merry Christmas," said Mr Ismay as they left.

Chapter II

In HER BLACK COAT, WITH HER BLACK HAIR PARTED IN THE
middle and lying long and gently over her shoulders, Mary
looked like a young novice. The white collar of her blouse
which peeped between the large black lapels of the old coat
could have been her nun's starched collar. She walked slowly,
always shy, her head inclined down, only risking a glance at
the shops every now and then, not wanting to block the
pavement by standing and staring, always sucked into the
life of her feelings, listening to her quiet thoughts, sensitive,
even timid, not wanting to be conspicuous.

She felt her stomach tighten nervously and she breathed
in slowly as Dr Dolan had told her to do. Her stomach
tightened again three or four times but she breathed in slowly
and walked steadily between the banked-up snow and the
stocked-up shops, aware of tinsel and holly, paper decorations, oranges, glistening wrapping-paper, carols coming
from tapes and transistors. At the Fountain, in the town
centre, three young men, already drunk, shouted—at no one

in particular. They wanted to make a noise. She picked up her step, wishing Joe had not left her: and glad he was different, not like them.

The town was small, however large it appeared to her, and soon she had passed through the shopping centre and was at the church square. The nervous pain had not quite gone and she began to worry that indeed her time might be coming though the child was not due for another two weeks. There was a bench in the church porch and she went to sit down. It was cold: her breath came out in small puffs of cloudy air. She burrowed her hands in her pockets and hoped that Joe had found a place. She could see how worried he was but there was so little she could do for him. However hard she tried to seize the moment when she could say the right thing, she was no longer strong enough. All her energy went inward, towards her child about whom she had such strange dreams that she dared tell no one about them.

"You'll starve to death there." Mary looked around in alarm, and relaxed only a little when she saw a red-faced man with white hair and a white beard standing beside her. Theatrically he took off the white beard, and the white hair came off too, revealing a yellowing crinkled bald head. He gave a little plump bow.

"Did the wig worry you? It's for Father Christmas at the Bazaar later on. I was trying it on in the vestry when I saw you freezing to death." He smiled. "Don't worry, I'm not a vicar. Come in and get warm. I won't bother you."

She followed him in. "The heating's on for Midnight Mass," he said. "It takes twelve hours to warm up and people expect it to be warm although it can't have been very hot in Bethlehem at that time of night. There's a pew over there right next to the big radiator and the pipes go under the seat." He guided her there and then trotted off. "You needn't pray if the spirit doesn't move you," he said.

She sat down and felt herself drop into a warm and secure contentment. Nearby was a stained-glass window showing the Madonna and Child. Mary looked at that peaceful face and the holy infant with his halo and found comfort. She, too, would soon smile down on a child.

"How do I look?" Father Christmas reappeared in full traditional regalia.

Mary laughed. "The white cushion shows through your buttons," she said.

He nodded and gazed down sadly at his large makeshift belly. "There isn't another cushion."

"You could move the two middle buttons over and then nobody would see anything," Mary suggested. "I'd do it in a couple of minutes if I had a needle and thread."

"Oh, I've got that," he said, "in one of the Lucky Dip parcels. I'll put 5p in to cover the cost." He was away and back again with the packet in no time. "I'll practise for tonight while you're working. Nice to be with nice people, isn't it?" Again his churchy shuffle took him off; before he went he noticed a likeness between the girl and the figure in the stained-glass window, but said nothing so as not to embarrass her.

He went to the organ and while he practised the well-known carols which the vicar had sensibly chosen for the Midnight Mass, Mary found comfort in the familiar activity of sewing on buttons. The warmth from the radiator and the music crept into her body and she felt it seep into her mind which dissolved into thoughts of the coming child.

Chapter III

AT THE OTHER END OF TOWN JOE WAS IN TROUBLE. MRS FELL was ill and not taking in lodgers. The little girl who had answered the door was suspicious and Joe had felt guilty. He walked slowly back towards the centre of the town, a striking man, tall, strongly built, with a face weathered and yet nervously alive, long fair hair thickly piling about his neck, openly worried. Strapped in a badly fitting raincoat, rather clumsy in his movements, he felt the first sickly alert of panic.

To him the town seemed full of people more clever, more successful, more enterprising than he was. All he had ever had to put against that had been his great physical strength and his innocent willingness: the one a source of respect, the other a target for jokes. But now he felt bereft of those powers. The hooter went and he knew Mary would be waiting in the Spotted Cow.

He had not thought things out and he did not want to face her. Unconsciously he slowed down. The crowds of workers began to emerge from the two short streets leading from the factory. The pubs were open. Outside the Black-a-Moor he saw Big Nick, who beckoned with that imperious nod it was impossible to refuse unless you wanted trouble.

As he walked across to the pub, the street lights on now, the snow glistening under the lights as if it were sweating, he remembered all his dealings with Big Nick. He was just a few years older than Joe but had a worldliness which Joe would never attain in a lifetime. Roughly conceived, carelessly delivered into the world, indifferently reared and casually educated, Nick had fallen into a world which needed his muscles and his obedience and had used the one to dent the other: fights, drunkenness, petty thefts, prison, assaulting two policemen, Durham Jail. And from Durham Jail he had emerged a man, a hard hero to those he worked with, villain to the many who feared him.

Around him had grown up the legends which glamorise all such tough men whose root trouble is connected with lack of love and lack of care. There could have been a Ballad of Big Nick—how he had taken on the Carlisle Race Gang on the staircase of a pub, breaking the bannisters to give himself weapons; how he had set rats in the saloon bar of another pub that had barred him; how he had married and left his wife the next day and months later smashed down the door of the house of the man she had gone to live with and had taken her back, only to reject her yet again; how he had brought up a fox and tried to tame a badger.

Joe knew all this and he also knew that Big Nick hated to be disobeyed in the smallest matter by those he considered his friends. Joe himself had become a friend on the building site when he had refused to carry Big Nick's hod for him. He would not be anybody's servant, he had said, and had waited for the fight. But Nick had seen his determination, sensed his strength and decided, he said, to "let him off". Someone else had carried the hod. Joe had been pronounced "a friend". From then on the rough pubs in which they drank, the fish-and-chip shop, the cafes and the betting shops considered him to be under Nick's protection and he had gone along with that, finding Nick an easygoing friend, once you accepted his leadership.

"We're goin' in for a drink," he said, his freshly shampooed hair shining under the street light; his face was thin, almost gaunt, his black suit shabby, his white shirt open at the neck.

"I have the wife waiting," Joe said.

"She'll wait." Nick turned and went into the pub. Joe, having glanced up and down the street, followed, justifying his betrayal by saying to himself that Nick or the landlord might know where they could find a room for the night.

Nick played darts. Shanghai. Joe was a brilliant pitcher, his game spoiled only by his slowness with the mathematics which interfered with his rhythm. Shanghai with its simple rules but difficult targets suited him perfectly. Nick knew this.

"We'll challenge any pair in the house," said Nick levelly. "Any pair in the house. Just for a drink. Nothing serious."

Joe wanted to bolt his drink and get up to see Mary, but he was weak and when two boozy teenagers, who had quit work that dinnertime and supped pints throughout the afternoon, came up to show the hairs on their chests and take up

Big Nick's challenge, he felt obliged to stay. Just for the one game.

"Middle for diddle," said Nick, and Joe threw a bull.

As he played, the shame of his wife waiting was temporarily alleviated by feelings of self-pity. What had he done to be picked out for such misfortune? He was sure he had not made her pregnant. And why was Mrs Fell unavailable just on this very day? The feathered darts drew short swift curves from hand to board and he drank too quickly for comfort.

"Double or quits," said Nick quickly, when they won the first game.

"I'll have to go," Joe heard his voice protesting feebly. "We need to find a place to stay for the night."

"Mr Briggs'll fix you up," Nick said confidently. Briggs was the landlord. "Got to give these lads a chance to get their own back. How about double or quits and a pound each on the side?"

"You're on," the boys chorused, flattered to be in the Big League.

"I'll ask him now," Joe said. Nick nodded.

"Mugs away?" the teenager enquired.

"Mugs away," Nick agreed solemnly, and like the thud of a hammer knocking in nails the darts went into the board.

But Mr Briggs was busy just then and Joe had to come back and finish the game. He could not go wrong.

"Tell you what," said Nick, as they won again, "forget about all bets. Five pounds a corner clear it all up. A Christmas bet, lads, what say?"

The teenagers dug their fists into their cheap jeans. They looked at their money, at each other and, finally, wordlessly, agreed. Joe had gone out of the room.

Mr Briggs was a conscientious "Mine Host", careful to keep his beer clean and anxious that everyone should have a good time. He knew distress when he saw it, and was copying down some addresses of places Joe might try, when Nick barged in. He waved down Joe's protests.

"They always wait," he said. "Besides, it wouldn't be fair to the two lads. They need a chance to get even. If you walk out now it'll look bad."

Joe found some consolation in insisting it was the very last game.

"Marriage is making you jittery," Nick observed. "Keep on top of it, son, or it will get you down."

The teenagers played much better this last time, with the twenty pound-coins lying on the table, and the game took much longer to finish. Again, though, they lost and were

angry when Joe insisted on leaving. They wanted a final game. He promised to return if he could.

Nick, too, was concerned but "The night is young," he said and as Joe left he looked fiercely at him and said, "He'll be back, won't you, Joe?" Joe did not reply. Mr Briggs' list of addresses was in his pocket and he rushed up the street. The cafe was shut.

"Don't rattle the door like that!" shouted Mr Robinson from across the street outside the bus-office. "That won't get you in."

"It's my . . . wife . . . I was supposed to meet her . . ."

"I've seen her trailing about, poor little lass. She needs looking after."

Indignation came easy to Mr Robinson. He could acceler-ate into righteous anger in two seconds over a child's attempt to evade legal payment on a bus journey; he would boil with moral fury if a bus-driver was late; impertinence from his staff would cause him to fulminate for hours. In Mary's situation was the perfect material for his kind of special relationship with the world. Joe was chastened.

"Where can she have gone?"

"I'd not be surprised if she'd put herself on the last bus back to where you came from."

"Did she?"

Mr Robinson paused for a cruel few moments and then with disappointment already shading into sympathy had to admit "No". Joe's relief softened him instantly; for on the other side of the irascibility was a sentimental, helpful soul who loved to bring aid and comfort. "No, she's the sort who would stick by you. I could tell that. You could see it in her eyes." Mr Robinson prided himself on his gift for seeing into people.

Joe felt his face scorch with shame. He had been playing darts, drinking, betting, and there she was alone, frightened, deserted, and now lost. The thought of this drove out all the other doubts and pains of the day. She needed him and he loved her. "That," he heard himself say to himself, as if an outside voice beyond his control were speaking to him, "that is all that matters—you must find her," the voice went on, "and look after her and help her with the child."

Being a Bus-Station Manager had made Mr Robinson accustomed to rapid decisions and soon he had a plan of action which would send Joe scurrying in one direction and three small boys hauled in to help, scattering in another direction. Mr Robinson wished they all had watches so that he could have said, "Synchronise watches", but you couldn't have everything. Joe set off for the Chinese fish-and-chip shop—"Where she would be warm, you see," Mr Robinson observed, "and able to sit down."

Chapter IV

MARY WAS ONLY A FEW YARDS FROM THE BUS-STATION, AT the Bazaar in the Parish Rooms to which she had been led by a stoutly re-buttoned Father Christmas who had seen her standing alone and cold outside the cafe and had over-ridden her objections, taking her with him.

If only she had not been worried about Joe, she would have loved it all. For here was the Christmas she had glimpsed in school concerts and heard about and read about in books.

A Christmas Child

Nice friendly people came into the large comfortable room, loudly kicking the snow off their shoes and giving out encouraging cries of appreciation at the decorations, the holly, the large Christmas tree and the decorated stalls which ran up and down in two rows, imitating a market.

She had been given a cup of tea and a scone, sat in a chair unobtrusively beside the stage which would only be used by the vicar (late as he always was) to announce the official opening (when it was half-over, as it always was) and she could feast on all the gentle joys of this comforting Bazaar where all the money would go to the local orphanage (Children's Home, it was called; but not by the older people of the town).

As witnesses to their need, the orphans themselves were there, some singing carols around the tree, others dashing about excitedly like ball boys at an important tennis match. Many, she noticed acutely, were as near tears as she herself at this vision of warmth which was so close to a promise of perfection, and so far from a part of their lives. One of them attached himself to Mary. She could feel his affection for her, instant, total, unconditional, pour out of his longing look. And all she had done was to ask him his name. He was about seven.

"John," he said. "I'm supposed to watch the coats."

"What for?" she asked. "None of these people would pinch anything, would they?"

"No," the boy agreed, as eager as she to idealise the company he was in. "But they have to have somebody to watch them. Somebody always does. Anyway, hardly anybody takes their coats off."

That satisfied both of them.

Soon she found that she was holding his hand.

There were so many questions she wanted to ask him— but dared not because the answers would be so big and she would not be able to do anything about it. This unusual caution was as clear as it was firm. Increasingly, as the afternoon had gone on, she had felt her mind, her feelings, her body even, though she knew this could not be really so, her blood, turning from the outside world, from others, from the surface of her skin and feeding the child.

"Can I get you a drink of orange?" John asked.

"No, I'm all right."

"Let me. I've got my own money. We got our money this morning."

"No thank you. Honest."

He accepted her decision reluctantly. The Home was in

the town, he told her, quite nearby, but they were only let out in a group and he wanted to go out on his own. That was his ambition—to be let out on his own one day.

Mr Miller (Father Christmas) came past ringing his bell and he gave her a specially kind look, rubbing his buttons. She could have cried for a moment and then she worried at the light-headedness which appeared to be possessing her.

"You can take what you want from the bran-tub free," said Mary. "Go on."

"I'd rather stay with you," the little boy said. "I want to get as much of you as I can. You're having a baby, aren't you?"

She looked away from him. His hair was short and fair and stiffly brushed up; his eyes were slightly crossed; he wore a grey sweater which was loose about his thin neck. He had the look of a starved hare, about to flee, nervous even of a caress. Mary gently squeezed his hand.

"Will you pretend to be my mother?" he whispered quietly and solemnly and then rushed on. "You needn't *do* anything or say anything, just sit like we are. But if I know you're pretending, I'll pretend."

He turned and looked at her almost savagely, his little blue eyes hard. She nodded and onto his white face there came the sudden thin gash of a smile. He sat at her feet like a dog and would not be tempted away by pleasure or by duty. With his eyes almost closed he mouthed a carol, silently . . .

Chapter V

Mr robinson's grand plan of campaign was in ruins. Two of the little boys failed to return, the third had found nothing. Joe, too, had failed to locate her and "What's worse," said Mr Robinson, "the left-luggage department" (a space under the counter) "closes officially at seven o'clock which is now. After that, you see, you're not insured but we can still be held responsible. It could be a very difficult situation should it arise."

Joe could not enter into Mr Robinson's troubles. He felt short of breath, weak in the legs, dry-throated, altogether distressed. Within a couple of minutes he was on the pavement with a case in each hand and Mr Robinson in a welter of apologies. He stood still and prayed hard, as hard as he could, that he would find her. Snow began to fall. He noticed the music coming from the Parish Rooms and followed it. And found her.

John gave her up as one who is used to giving up what he wants. But Mary would not let the parting be without

37

meaning. As Joe had not yet told her of the failure of his search for a lodging, she was full of hope and certainty and this she shed on John as she took him to the "As New" toy stall and, outwitting his attempt to buy nothing, got him a small red engine which ran along the ground when you wound it up with a key. The little boy held it as if it were a casket of precious ointment. John shepherded her out of the room.

Father Christmas waved and rang his bell. Other people waved as if she had known them for years. "Merry Christmas" came across the room to her like a talisman. On the steps outside they stepped aside for the vicar who was trotting in with his watch in front of his eyes like the White Rabbit.

"I'll like it here," she said and then, daringly, in the dark alley which led to the Parish Rooms, she kissed Joe on the lips, feeling the soft snow melt.

"Thank you," she said.

"What for?"

"Bringing me here."

He hesitated. It pained him to deliver any unpleasant or unwelcome news to anyone: to tell Mary that he had not found lodgings needed all his nerve.

"What's wrong?" she asked, helping him, understanding.

He told her, falteringly, ending by opening the list of addresses given by Mr Briggs. The white sheet fluttered between them like a small flag of truce.

"I'll go back inside and ask there," said Mary, emboldened by the memory of the warmth of the place and made decisive by the sharpening of needs her body was feeling. "They'll help."

"They don't know us," Joe argued, shy, still shy in spite of the urgency, and still afraid to impose.

"They're good people," said Mary. "Church people. Well-dressed."

It was partly, then, to show off her new-found wealth of good companionship that induced Mary to return to the Bazaar. Father Christmas came across to her immediately, but swift as he was, John beat him there and took one of Mary's hands passionately in his own, blushing with immeasurable pleasure.

"We have nowhere to stay the night," Mary explained to Mr Miller. "We wondered if you knew anybody could give us lodgings."

As soon as she had finished her sentences, Mary was aware that Mr Miller's eyes glazed, then turned thoughtful, and then settled on Joe who, red-faced and raw-looking from the couple of pints and the beating about the town, presented a figure of no distinction whatever.

"This will be your husband?"

"Yes," she smiled proudly.

"Why haven't you got a place before now?" Mr Miller's question was sharp.

"We were let down," said Mary, helping Joe. "We were . . . let down."

"This is very inconvenient," Mr Miller said with such irritation that Mary wished she had never asked. "I mean. After seven o'clock on Christmas Eve. Everybody with their preparations made. Families about them. Why don't you go back to where you came from?"

"The last bus has gone," Joe said. "And besides, we want to stay here."

"Stay where you are," Father Christmas spoke with what he intended to be kindly severity, "and I'll see what I can do."

As the red-robed figure went around the warm, busy room, Mary felt herself looked over, appraised, judged, by dozens of eyes she had until then thought friendly. Everyone seemed to shake their heads. She felt faint and leaned back against Joe.

"You could stay with me," said John, vehemently, "but they wouldn't let you!"

"Please," she whispered to Joe, "please, let's go."

"Not while he's trying to get us a place, surely," Joe countered, wanting to be fair.

"Please."

It was this which had joined them from the beginning and set them apart; this fearful understanding of each other's embarrassment. Joe could understand the pressure on Mary and he picked up their cases and stepped outside.

The little boy came out with them and shivered silently at the snow. "Let me come with you," he said before they had taken a step. "I won't say anything. I don't eat much. I can be useful. Please take me with you."

"They wouldn't let us," Mary replied on that note of simple bitter truth the boy had learned he could not fight. "And they would put us in jail for trying." She paused. "We'll come and see you when we've found a place."

"Promise?" demanded the small boy.

"Promise."

"Cross your heart and hope to die."

"Yes." She kissed him on the cheek. "Merry Christmas."

The boy watched them walk away.

Then began their pilgrimage around the town. The snow fell intermittently. There was nowhere for Mary to stay and wait but the pubs which were full and the fish-and-chip shop which was rowdy. She did not want to be parted from Joe again. Drunks, cheerful generally, but with the ominous uncertainty of men beyond normal constraints, would stumble into the snow drifts and back out, moving along erratically, hands stuffed in pockets. Last-minute carol singers infiltrated the dark streets and yards where Mr Briggs' address book took them, but wherever they turned, there was no room.

And Mary knew that her time would soon come.

The last address took them to Water Street and to reach it they had to pass the back of the dance hall where the Orientals were playing. Mary tugged Joe's arm to stop and they stood for a moment, outside the back door. Joe with the two suitcases like dead weights on his hands, Mary leaning into him, pretending to listen to the music while she took time to rest, to suppress the trembling she had felt before it overcame her.

"They're good, aren't they?" Joe said. "I had one of their records." For the Orientals had been famous in their time and long ago even got a silver disc, until they had decided, as their leader had put it to the Press, "to follow their own star, go out into the world and come back with something New".

They were just about to move on when Big Nick and the two teenagers whom he appeared to have adopted for the night, came around the corner with comical stealth and made for the back door which Nick assaulted savagely, all stealth forgotten, trying to rip the thing down and get in free. "I'll not pay a pound," he kept muttering. "Not a bloody penny. What're you two bloody lookin' at?" It was to Joe and Mary he spoke, having suddenly noticed them, and at the two of them he aimed his alcoholic body. The teenagers stumbled behind him. "Joe! Where've you been? It's my old pal Joe!"

"We waited for that other game," one of the teenagers said. "We waited and waited. Didn't we?"

His appeal met with emphatic agreement.

"Waited and waited," he went on. "Waited and waited. Didn't we?"

This time there was no seconding.

"My old pal Joe!" said Nick, coming down to the heart of the matter and slamming a large hand on Joe's shoulder. "Give us a hand with this door, Joe." He turned to his new friends. "Joe's as strong as a bloody bullock. He could split that door open with his bare head—couldn't you, Joe?"

Like a proud father, Nick beamed all about him and then tugged at Joe to accompany him to the impeding door.

"We can't," said Joe. "We're looking for somewhere to stay."

"Stay with me," Nick spoke promptly. "Always stay with me. Send the little lady down there now. No bother. Just tell my old woman I sent you and any trouble, she'll get one around the bloody teeth. She'll be glad to see you. Reminds me. Christmas present." He dipped his hand into his clothes and pulled out a large and crumpled box of Black Magic which he thrust at Mary. "Give her this. She knows I always get her this. The mother," he felt compelled to explain. "That's who I'm talking about. Only woman worth fighting for is your mother. Right, Joe?"

"We have to be on our way, Nick."

"Not before we get in this dance. And I'm against paying a pound on principle—see what I mean? Granted."

Nick was royally drunk, gloriously, wickedly, drunk, happily winding himself up for the trouble he intended to stir all about him that night.

But he had all his wits about him still and when the police car came slowly around the corner, they found the two teenagers hammering hopelessly on the door and Nick, his arm around Joe, standing at attention, joining in with the song coming through the wall from the Orientals. The teenagers seemed glad to be taken away; initiation, it seemed, complete. A police-cell on Christmas Eve was something they would be a little proud of until their strength began to ebb.

"Your husband was always lucky for me," Nick said to Mary, ruffling Joe's hair. "He's my lucky charm."

"I'm going now, Nick," said Joe.

"No, you're not."

"I am."

"Lend us a quid." Nick paused. "Tax," he said. Joe knew the implications if he did not pay this "tax". For Mary's sake he would make no protest. He handed it over. Nick dropped it into his breast-pocket and swiftly went away.

"What a horrible man!" Mary sobbed and Joe felt her shake against him. Her face was cold. His own body was warm but he was afraid for Mary with her extra life to comfort.

"Nick's all right. He *did* offer to put us up."

"If you'd accepted—I couldn't have gone."

"I knew." He paused. "I was tempted to take it."

"I felt that."

"It would solve our problem, Mary."

"No. Not that."

"Well, there's only Mrs Henderson left to try on this list. It should be round past the cemetery."

Mrs Henderson said right away that she had no room but she invited them in and fussed over them, gave them tea and listened to their story, noted Mary's condition and eventually "popped out to see what she could do", leaving them warm, almost weak with the sudden cosiness, side by side like lovers, on the settee, watching the choirs singing on television and imagining what life could be like if they should ever have enough to come into a home as pleasant as this. For Mrs Henderson—as she had explained—was a widow and with the insurance after her husband's death, she had bought herself "some good furniture. All my life I'd wanted good furniture, I'd wanted nothing else, really, and so I said, Elsie, it's now or never." She would go and see a relative, she said.

"We can't stay in this town," Joe said, out of the blue. "After you've had the baby, we'll move on."

"Why?"

"Something about it. As we were walking around looking for a room tonight. Something said to me—this is the place for the birth, but after that—move on."

"Where?"

"South. Far away from here. Where we'll be safe," he heard himself saying.

She took his hand and accepted what he said. She would have followed him to the ends of the earth. Though they sat, a confused and confounded couple, late on Christmas Eve in a bleak northern settlement, still without shelter for the night and about to enter into the mystery which would alter their lives for ever, though they could be described as foolish, ignorant, forlorn, though they could be pitied for lack of foresight and condemned for lack of common sense, they seemed to be sure that something outside and above them-selves bound them and would secure them even against the indifferent snow.

"Well," said Mrs Henderson, red-faced from the cold and excited by her success, "I've done the best I can and though it isn't much it'll be the best you can find. Mr Briggs," she announced rather proudly, "in the pub, was my dead husband's brother-in-law, and though all his rooms are taken tonight by them Orientals, he has a place in the back-yard that his son—this is, James, the eldest, turned into a . . . well, place he could work in when he was . . . what they call 'studying' for college. Put a bed in it. Blocked up the holes. Bits of carpet on the floor. You see," she hesitated, "it used to be a stable. And in the loft upstairs, Mr Briggs has his budgies—but they won't disturb you. Anyway. He didn't want to mention it before but I persuaded him." She smiled. "He says he'll put a paraffin stove in when the pub closes and—well . . ." She was suddenly conscious of the poverty of the offer.

"That will be good enough for us," said Mary. "Thank you."

They had to wait until the pub closed and so when they left Mrs Henderson's, the sombre lines of people moving through the winter streets for Midnight Mass were already on the march.

Someone ran up to them, out of breath, old, his face in a rictus of apology.

"Did you find somewhere?" They looked at him. "Father Christmas without the fancy dress . . . Mr Miller in civvies . . ." He flapped a hand to indicate the bell he had rung. "Ding Ding! You didn't give us a chance. We would have worked something out. Of course it would have meant you splitting up for the night . . ."

"We found somewhere for both of us, thank you."

"Oh good. Good, good," said Mr Miller, happy to be relieved. "Oh *good*! Well. Merry Christmas!"

Mrs Briggs showed them to the stable. Though almost exhausted after a hectic night in the pub, she chatted to them and offered them a Christmas drink and made them feel welcome. Outside the window were fields deep in snow, empty, the cattle well in for the night, only the sheep huddled against the dry stone walls on the illuminated hills.

"It isn't too bad," she said ruefully. "It's clean, and warm, and weatherproof."

"It suits us grand," said Joe, but when she had left, he turned to Mary, his eyes suddenly tingling with tears. "I should have done better than this for you. I'm sorry, Mary."

She kissed him consolingly but in truth she was far away from him because she knew the child would come soon now and all her life went into it.

The boy was born there just before the church bells had rung out for the first communion. And the doctor, who had cursed the call on this of all days, felt his heart lift with happiness at the aura of the lovely child as it snuggled peacefully against its mother's breast. Above the little town, at dawn, seen for miles, there rose the morning star.

The wonder of the birth was soon around the town and people came to give something to the child. The Orientals,

uncommonly moved by the event, each gave a ring before heading back east to their city.

Mr Robinson had sent word up to the village, and friends of Joe and Mary, farm-labourers, shepherds, came down to see if they could help; and somehow John too heard the news and wriggled out of the Home to find the place where the baby was born, and he emptied his pockets and gave the new child all he had.

For life had come out of darkness once again. The miracle was there to be seen and believed.